William Strong

For my loving wife Daniele, and for the next
level of human exploration.
And for you, for being a part of the Mars
Journey. Ad Mars et Ultra (To Mars and
Beyond).

I0539078

Mars Journey: Call to Action: Book 1

William Strong

Mars Journey: Call to Action: Book 1

William Strong

Formerly known as Bill Hargenrader

Sign up for updates on new books, Mars
SciFi, science and more at:
http://marsjourney.info

An Epic Journeys Entertainment Book
Philadelphia

Mars Journey: Call to Action: Book 1

Mars Journey: Call to Action is a work of fiction. Names, characters, places, and incidents either are the product of the author's imagination, or are used fictitiously. Any resemblance to actual persons, living, or dead, events, or locales, is entirely coincidental.

Mars Journey, and Epic Journeys are Trademarks of Epic Journeys Entertainment, LLC.

ISBN: 0692554394

ISBN-13: 978-0692554395

Table of Contents

Part 1 - T-Minus 7 years

Chapter 1

3.5Gs of crushing pressure exerted itself on the bodies and organs of the two astronauts geared up in their orange flight suits and locked into takeoff position inside the compact spacecraft atop the rapidly ascending rocket. These two veterans of space-flight were used to these conditions. What they were not used to was the dangerous rescue mission they were embarking on—one that had never been attempted before.

Three days earlier, the crew of the *Pisces III*, one of Earth's first full-sized commercial space stations, stopped transmitting. To make matters worse, the Pisces was losing orbit rapidly. Thousands of techs, engineers, and analysts from around the globe, working on this problem around the clock, came up with the plan that was now being set in motion at 28,000 kilometers per hour.

As Brent Carlson, commander of the mission, waited for the vibrations in his skull to subside, he recalled the words of NASA chief Mike Johnson a day earlier as he had addressed him and his pilot Calvin Williams.

"We are sending two of NASA's—actually, two of Earth's—bravest and best astronauts up in our most advanced spacecraft to rescue the crew of the Pisces," Johnson had said. "This has never been done before, and I have 100 percent faith that you will pull this off for the sake of the crew of the Pisces and for the honor of the astronaut corps. The world is watching. God speed."

Not too much pressure there, Brent thought.

Their spacecraft reached a constant velocity some 220 kilometers above the Earth, and the familiar feeling of microgravity set in. From here they would have just over four hours before the Wyvern completed its five automated engine burns that would bring them in for their rendezvous with the Pisces.

Brent and Williams got the signal from ground control to take off their helmets. As Brent removed his, he felt the heat of the capsule air and breathed in the familiar aroma of the cockpit: body odor, and motor oil—like a cross between a locker room and an auto shop.

"How you making out over there, Hulk Junior?" asked Brent.

Williams shot him a look. Brent had given him the nickname because of Williams' musclebound, five-foot-seven frame. Normally, excessive muscle was a detriment to space operations, but Williams had an ease of movement gained from years of climbing in and out of the cockpit as a Marine Corps fighter jet pilot. He was one of the few African Americans to make more than four trips to space, a feat he was not shy of bringing up repeatedly.

"Doing just fine, Wolverine," Williams retorted. "You?"

Wolverine was the nickname Williams had chosen to mock Brent's *occasional* temper flare up. Brent, with his short cropped brown hair, and lean athletic build, actually kind of liked the label, since he thought it matched him well with the mammal known for its strength and ferocity out of proportion to its size.

"Rock solid here," said Brent. "Only two of Earth's finest, ready to save the day."

"Actually, that reminds me," said Williams. "I know why they're sending me, being practically the best damn pilot alive. Still haven't figured out why they sent you though."

Brent let out a laugh. "I'm just here to make sure the helmet fits over that big head of yours, buddy." He extended his fist over to Williams, who bumped it, completing their orbital insertion good luck ritual.

"Alright, let's get ourselves mentally prepped for this mission," said Brent. "Only four hours till contact."

"Roger that," said Williams.

It really wasn't a mystery why Brent was here. Years ago Brent had been a child prodigy excelling in the field of astrophysics. He possessed a unique super computer-like mind that could mentally build and breakdown objects in his head, run multiple simulations on those objects, and tweak minor details to get variations on results, allowing him to see things others couldn't. While 13 year old kids in his neighborhood were lucky if they could identify a constellation, Brent was discovering galaxies. Brent gave up on the safe and boring path of academia, for a life of adventure in the Army, and eventually the Astronaut Corp...

But there was no use thinking about that now; these were distractions.

Funny what your mind thinks of when you're hurtling towards a structure 100 times your size that is quite literally falling into the planet, where one false move can send you spiraling out into the vast void of space... thought Brent.

Brent used that daunting visual to focus himself. He reviewed the dossier in his head. He ran through the crew members, their faces, and backgrounds. He ran through the list of potential problems. There were many. There was potentially an oxygen shortage, power outage, biological contaminants, pressurization issues, you name it. There were so many possibilities, and only so much time left. They were risking their lives in a maneuver that had only been invented yesterday.

Normally a rapid orbital rendezvous required extreme precision coordination from both the spacecraft and the space station. With the *Pisces* out of commission, that meant the Wyvern would have to bear the full brunt of the adjustment maneuvers. A seemingly impossible scenario.

In a bold move, Ken Solum, CEO of NewSpace Enterprises, personally guaranteed the Wyvern could handle it. After NASA agreed, the upgraded maneuver code was uploaded to the Wyvern spacecraft on the fly, and now here they were, circling the planet, moving closer to their rescue attempt.

A few hours later the two astronauts felt the last of the automated engine burns that took them out of phasing orbit and into the path of the *Pisces*. Brent continued to run visualizations of the rescue mission procedures. He looked back over the Wyvern's interior. Seven seats in total, two for him and Williams. One for each of the five crew members of the Pisces. If they were still alive.

"Holy crap!" said Williams. "Check that out, Carlson."

Brent looked up to a display monitor in the Wyvern showing a magnified view of their target.

On the screen, the football field-sized *Pisces* space station loomed overhead in the distance. No lights emanating. Half of the solar array hanging off its moorings at the wrong angle. If it weren't for being on the bright side of the Earth, they wouldn't have been able to see it.

"Whoa, she looks dead," said Brent.

"If there's anyone alive on there, we'll get them out," said Williams.

"Agreed," Brent said. "Alright, take it in, Williams. You're the best damn pilot we have. That's why you're here. Make it happen."

And just like that, Williams snapped out of any semblance of a normal human; man and machine had become one. His gaze set, his hands on the controls, guiding the Wyvern ever closer. Foot pedals applying thrust. With one eye on the proximity gauge and one on the visual display, they made their way ever closer to the *Pisces* docking port. They navigated with the apparent ease that only a skilled and time tested pilot could, through an obstacle course of debris, and around the solar array panel that was blocking the normal entry route.

This guy is good, Brent thought. Then, Brent's focus went to the docking procedures.

Since the *Pisces* was seemingly having electric generation issues, they had rigged the Wyvern with an extra power source. They would reverse the energy feed toward the *Pisces* and, in essence, act as a massive battery to power the station's auxiliary systems to assist in the rescue.

KA-THUNK!

The Wyvern vibrated lightly as Williams executed a bull's-eye docking.

"That's my Ace!" shouted Brent.

Over their headsets, ground control gave Williams a more formal congratulations.

"That was almost too easy," said Williams with a self-satisfied smile.

"Easy big guy, we're just getting warmed up here," said Brent. "Now, let's go rescue some civvies."

Chapter 2

Brent and Williams unharnessed themselves and floated in zero G over to the Wyvern dock hatch where they waited for the automated coupling to complete. The *Pisces* schematics showed backup battery on the oxygen generation units, so they had anticipated the results being 50 percent of optimal. If it was low to zero, they would quickly reattach their helmets and prepare for *R* operations. Thankfully, there was no need for that, since the display showed positive at 80 percent.

That's higher than it should be... thought Brent, but the hiss of the hatch opening broke his concentration.

The Pisces docking port opened into darkness.

Brent stared into the void as his eyes adjusted. Then, suddenly, a figure careened wildly toward them through the blackness, shouting gibberish.

That's not gibberish, Brent realized. *It's French!*

It was Andrea Martine, the lead civilian scientist. Her red hair and fashion model-like facial features would be hard to mistake for anyone else, even despite her current disheveled appearance.

"Merci, merci, you must help the others," she said, grabbing Brent by the suit. "We thought we were done for."

"That's why we're here," said Brent, gripping her hands as she looked into his eyes.

"Thank God," she said. "Thank you. Thank you so much." She tried to pull Brent closer, and Brent found himself holding her back.

"Ma'am, ma'am," Williams interjected.

"Oh, yes," Andrea said, wiping a tear from the corner of her eye.

"Where is the rest of your crew?" continued Williams.

"Jean Louis and crew at your service," came a French-accented voice from the dock doors.

They turned to see the remaining four members of the *Pisces* lined up at the hatch.

"We figured that a rescue via space vessel was the highest probability, so we gathered here," said Jean Louis.

"That was a good plan," said Brent. "It's far less risky for us to have to board the *Pisces*. Come on. Let's get you all strapped in so we can get you safely home."

The lights in the entryway began to flicker. All at once, they turned on.

Andrea looked up at the lights with a look of shock. "How is that possible?" she said.

"We are powering the station temporarily," said Brent. "We thought it might be necessary."

"Smart thinking," Andrea began, but she was cut off by Jean Louis.

"Wait—power is on now?" he said. "I can get my experiments that were on emergency lock down! It will only take a minute."

Before Brent or Williams could say anything, Jean pushed off and floated his way back on to the *Pisces*.

From behind, an alarm started blaring.

Brent turned to look at a gauge on the Wyvern console. "Not good," he said. "We are dropping altitude faster than the predictions."

"Why?" asked Williams.

"Must be when we reversed the energy flow," said Brent. "Some of the structural alignment thrusters kicked in... We're rapidly descending."

"Roger that," said Williams. "Lock these guys in. I'm going after our runner."

Brent nodded his okay, but then, all of a sudden, his world appeared to move in slow motion. Brent's hyper-speed mind had taken over. Something wasn't right. The rapid descent. The oxygen levels at 80 percent instead of 50 percent... Layers of schematics, blueprints, conversations with techs and engineers ran through his mind in rapid succession.

Andrea floated in front of him. "Is there anything I can do to help?"

Brent didn't respond. He was still locked in his trance-like thought, running the scenario again and again in his mind, changing tiny details and small variations. Maybe it was nothing.

Stay focused, this is important, a voice spoke up in his mind. It was the voice of his wife Shayla—the internal voice that he used to keep himself calm in stressful situations.

He had been thinking of the *Pisces* in its entirety; but now he focused in on individual modules, their components, and how they interacted. How they each affected one another, and—

Wait. There it is—No!

Brent, startled from his trance, shouted, "Williams! Wait! If you go after him, we all die! We have to get out of here *now*!"

"I'm not leaving him behind," Williams shouted back and continued to make his way back to the *Pisces*.

Sorry, my friend. No way I'm going to let that happen.

Brent quickly searched for a way to stop him. Williams wasn't responding to commands. He wasn't the type to respond to threats. A blow from the fire extinguisher to Brent's right could kill him. Any punch that Brent threw could break his hand and was no guarantee of disabling Williams. Williams was far too strong to grapple.

I'll have to put him to sleep.

Brent narrowed his eyes on the back of Williams' neck. By now, he was halfway through the vessel docking bay.

Brent grasped the side of the seat he was next to for stability, planted both his feet on the side of it, and propelled himself forward as he floated in zero G on a precise trajectory for Williams. At the last second, Williams sensed Brent's approach, but it was too late. Brent's arm was already snaked around Williams' neck, wrapping around to clasp his own arm. He placed his hand on the top of Williams' head in a perfectly executed rear naked choke.

And Brent squeezed as hard as he could.

Excellent technique. Ideal leverage. Williams should be out cold in three, two, one...

Williams defied the average and, tightening the knotty muscles in his neck, managed to stay conscious. He thrashed and elbowed back into Brent's ribs to little effect. He reached back and tried to punch Brent in the face but missed awkwardly. Brent was using the benefit of weightlessness to nullify his friend's incredible strength.

Former friend, probably, he thought. *I don't see us staying friends after this.*

Finally, Williams went limp.

Brent sensed the seconds ticking down fast. He grabbed Williams under both armpits like a lifeguard with a drowning victim, then found purchase with his feet on a rung and launched them both sailing back through the Wyvern bay.

Brent clipped his head hard on the top of the hatch bulwark.

That's gonna leave a mark.

As he sailed past Andrea he shouted to her, "Get that hatch sealed!"

Andrea, with tears rimming her eyes now, shook her head no. Behind her, the rest of the crew were buckled into their seats, looking nearly as confused as they were terrified. Brent muscled Williams' limp body into a seat and threw a harness strap over his shoulder.

"Get that hatch shut now, or you kill the rest of them!"

"I—I can't."

BOOM!

A massive reverberation rocked through the vessel, vibrating the very air. Brent's hyper-speed mind identified it as the engine compartment.

"*Now!*" he shouted at Andrea.

She obeyed and pushed off towards the hatch to close it as Brent made his way to the cockpit chair, taking time to buckle only one of his harness straps. Out of the corner of his eye, he saw down the Pisces docking bay. Jean Louis was returning, his hands full of documents, his face fearful. He started to shout something, but he fell out of view as Andrea closed the hatch.

"I am so very sorry, my love," she whispered just barely loud enough for Brent to hear.

BOOM.

The Wyvern capsule was rocked again by another explosion. It was a sound Brent's mind could only imagine as the tearing down of a skyscraper or the rending of an airplane in half. It ripped through the capsule. His hands were rapidly flitting across the touchscreen display, disengaging the connector protocols.

"Buckle up!" he shouted to Andrea, motioning with his head to the seat next to where Williams was lying, unconscious still. "And get him fully strapped in."

Andrea, face gaunt and distant as a shell-shocked soldier, moved forward to comply with the order. Brent looked to the heads-up display that showed minute separation.

Not happening fast enough! We're dead if we don't get some more thrust...

Brent activated a separate console display used for the six reentry thruster rockets to slow the Wyvern down for landing—not the minute and detailed thrusters used for space ops. He held his breath, hit the button, and waited for the acceleration.

Nothing.

Nothing happened. He looked down and saw the screen was visually crossed off, displaying the words: Action Prohibited.

"Action prohibited!" Brent shouted. "The hell it is! This is my Wyvern!"

Brent pushed aside the console and reached down between his feet to pull up the manual controls. He locked it in place, found the six red panel covers for the thruster switches, and flicked them up.

He was about to flip the switches when he heard screams from behind him. He looked back to see the rescued crew staring out at the viewport window. Half of the *Pisces III* was on fire, the translucent blue fire that Brent had only seen in space experiments at small scale. From this close up it was both mesmerizing and terrifying, and it was spreading rapidly to where the main oxygen tanks were housed.

"My God..." Brent said. Then, he flipped the switches.

Full thrust buried them all back in their seats just as the *Pisces* oxygen tanks exploded. The Wyvern accelerated forward, chased by an ever-expanding fireball threatening to engulf them.

Chapter 3

Minutes later, after narrowly escaping incineration, Brent shut down the thrusters at a safe distance from the wreckage of the *Pisces* in order to conserve the rest of their fuel for landing. He reengaged the Wyvern's automated controls and was running a diagnostic on the hull. Heat shields were good for heat; not debris from exploding spaces stations.

Brent unbuckled his harness and floated over to the porthole view to try and see the *Pisces*—what was left of her. She was a smoldering hulk in the distance, only visible as the smaller debris around it still glowed an eerie pale blue like space's version of a glowing red ember from a campfire.

Andrea joined Brent at the porthole view, watching the space station go down.

"All my life's work," she said. "My partner..."

Brent looked at her, knowing nothing he could say would help. She was lucky to be alive. *He* was lucky to be alive. They all were. But sometimes being lucky wasn't enough to take away your pain over losing someone close to you.

Brent looked back as Williams began to stir in his seat. Brent's eyes drifted to the empty seat where Jean Louis should have been.

This is going to change things...

T-Minus 6 Years

Chapter 4 - Location: New York City, United States

The floor of the United Nations building was a wild, tumultuous scene. A raucous, unruly congregation raised their voices loudly as they began to process the announcement made by the Professor of Foreign Relations from Stanford University. Shayla Carlson stood in the center of the floor with over 200 dignitaries from foreign nations looking down at her with skepticism, and in many cases, disgust.

Well, that didn't go over too well, her expression said as she looked back to her husband Brent.

At the U-shaped table, some distance in front of Shayla's podium, the jowls of U.S. Ambassador Smith shook as he reached forward to adjust his microphone downward.

"Mrs. Carlson," he began. "My apologies. I meant Dr. Carlson. What you are saying is that we pool our resources, and simply dissolve all barriers to technology sharing across all nations, in order to—to... take a trip to Mars? Why in the world now? Especially after the devastating tragedy that befell the Pisces. What has changed? And why would we ever trust our secrets with..." He shot a look at Ambassador Jiang from China. "With nations who have proven untrustworthy?"

At that, a new chorus of consternation arose, and several of the members at the table swiftly stood in immediate protest, turning and shouting.

"A nation such as yours has utterly no grounds to preach to others of trustworthiness!" leveled Jiang.

Many more had now risen, and the scene threatened to turn into complete discord when Brent Carlson took the mic.

Brent cleared his throat. "Hem, hem... Sorry to interrupt this... discourse. But I couldn't help but say something."

"You do not have the right to take the floor," said Smith. "Security!"

Brent looked around nervously and spotted a guard advancing on his position.

"Let her husband speak," shouted someone from the surrounding stands, followed by more calls of the same. Quickly the chorus rose throughout the chambers.

"Seems your occupation as an astronaut has garnered you a bit of celebrity in these halls," said Smith, contemplating the political fallout from denying Brent the right to speak. The guard looked to Smith, who shook his head. "Okay, you have two minutes, Mr. Carlson, but get to the point."

"Ah, well, hmm," said Brent, noticing the hundreds of eyes fixed upon him, and realizing that he really didn't know exactly what he was going to say.

Shayla cocked her head and leaned in. "My husband can fly at the tip of a twenty-story rocket but can't talk to these old, fat blowhards?" she whispered.

Brent gave a light chuckle. She always could make him laugh. A half grin formed at the edge of his mouth, the one she knew well—the one that said he was about to get into some mischief or trouble. Or both.

He began, "Thank you, now, my wife is actually the smart one with the master plan. I am just the worker bee astronaut who spent over a year in space. Just to let you know how not smart I am, did you know that it takes fifty people to plan out my day when I am aboard the International Space Station? Fifty people! That means I am, like, one-fiftieth as smart as a regular person."

This raised some laughs from the audience.

"I'm wearing a suit today," he continued. "It took me about thirty minutes to put on. But when I'm flying around the planet at 17,000 miles per hour, or outside one of our launch vehicles, it takes me a full four hours to get my suit on, and that's with someone else helping! Clearly, I'm lacking in intelligence somewhere."

The timing was just right and caused more laughter. Ambassador Jiang sat back and gave a quizzical but interested sidelong glance. Ambassador Smith just scowled and tapped his watch theatrically.

"Right, then," said Brent. "So, I didn't come here to regale you with tales of my stupidity. As a matter of fact, I just came to support my wife, who has spent the last seven years painstakingly building a plan that could send us to the furthest reaches of space, where we have never been before. This is her show, and the only reason I took the mic is because I couldn't bear to see the laughs, the jeers, the insults at such a masterfully crafted and thoroughly vetted plan."

"Mr. Carlson," Smith interrupted, "this plan has already been disproven. Time and time again, history has shown that when we want to get something done, whether it's traveling to a new continent or mapping out new territory, it's been for financial gain. And when we went to the moon, it was because of competition. Your plan has none of that."

"That's where you're wrong. What's not written in those papers, what's not written down, is the human spirit. And not just the human spirit, but also our evolving humanity.

I've been dreaming of going to Mars ever since I was a kid, and even as an astronaut in a country that has a plan to go, my heart breaks every time a program gets pushed back, every time a timeline is extended by five years. There's an old saying that goes something like this: You should only have the goal of being a millionaire, not for the money you will make, but for the person you will have to become in order to make it. That's what traveling to Mars is really all about. It's a challenge on a global scale, and it's a goal of humanity to become an interplanetary species, not just to say that we did it, not just to begin building a secondary home to ensure species survival in the case of a cataclysmic asteroid strike. No, it is a goal for humanity, for who we will have to become as a people to pull this off!"

Some cheers rose from the crowd. Ambassador Smith eyed the room, visibly uncomfortable with how the tide was changing.

"They say we can't do it alone," Brent continued. "I'm looking around at nations right in front of me who have the technology, the will, and the funding, and are just looking for someone to pull them together. They say we can't go to Mars unless there is a space race. A competition to pit ourselves against one another. I say there is a competition. And that competition is against those who say we can't do it. It's against our past-selves. Our past-selves who committed genocide and slave trading. We are better than those people, just like we are better than the people who need a space race to make this work. There is no place for that in our future. My challenge to you, and you, and you." He pointed to individuals in the crowd. "And my challenge to everyone out there isn't how to create a space race. It's how to get the human race to space, to Mars, and beyond. Will we be better than our past-selves? Will we repeat the same tragic mistakes? Or will we seize the moment to unite for this, our greatest cause? It's up to you to make the decision. That's really all I have to say. Thank you. Ad Mars et Ultra."

The chamber erupted in cheers, and Ambassador Smith smacked his gavel down hard, again and again. Ambassador Jiang leaned forward and slowly nodded as a smile spread across his face.

Shayla turned to Brent. "Wow! Where did that come from?"

"I don't know!" he said, shaking his head incredulously.

She pulled him down to her face and kissed him hard, oblivious to the crowded room around them.

Chapter 5

Outside the UN building, a man dressed in a black suit, a silver tie, and black, horn-rimmed glasses made his way hurriedly through the crowd to his limo waiting at the curb. He let out a sigh before he got in. He knew what to expect, but he didn't know what he would do.

He opened the door, and the secure, red phone in the middle console rang. He scuffed the top of his head in his hurry to sit down. As the door closed behind him, his eyes locked on the phone.

What should I say?

The phone rang again.

Don't let it ring a third time. Just pick up!

He picked it up with a split second to spare. He was met with the familiar electronic tones and hissing of the cyber-encryption scrambling protocol.

Alright, alright, you'll think of something.

And when that was finished, he was greeted by the operator.

"Yes, I'm ready to be patched through," he told the operator.

When he was transferred, he was surprised to hear the voice on the other end sounded even more enraged then he had imagined.

"Yes, sir…" he said. "I know, sir. That did not go as planned at all."

He moved the phone away from his ear to keep the shouts from the other end from damaging his eardrum.

"Of course we have contingency plans." He paused to listen, holding the phone closer now, as the voice on the other end shifted to a lower tone. He liked that tone even less. He'd heard it used on a colleague before. Shortly after, that colleague had been sent on a deep-cover assignment and hadn't been heard from since.

"We had no idea Brent Carlson was going to speak, let alone sway the entire Security Council to vote like that," he explained. "Even Ambassador Smith reluctantly…"

The voice on the other end interrupted him. His face dropped, and he became acutely aware that he might not get a second chance. His hand went to rest on his holster, his eyes leveled on the divider that separated him from the driver, half expecting it to lower at any second.

How easy would it be to take me out in this armored, soundproof car?

He snapped back to the conversation, realizing he had been asked a question.

"Sir!" he said. "I will make sure this gets taken care of. I will do whatever it takes—*whatever it takes*—to make this right and ensure your anonymity. I have a plan that I am putting into place as we speak."

There was no response on the other end for what seemed like a full minute. Just as he was about to ask if the connection was still good, he got his response.

"Yes, sir. I understand completely, sir."

The phone went dead. He let it hang there in his lap for a minute, too stunned to move. He'd been given an ultimatum. He had to make this go away, or he would go away. Permanently.

Well, at least I have one more chance. Better make it count.

He hung up the phone and pushed the intercom for the driver.

"Start driving," he said, and released the button.

"Where to, Mr. White?" replied the driver.

"Just drive!" he screamed into the intercom, jabbing his index finger on the button so hard and fast that his fingernail bent back and tore off.

As the limo began to drive away, he said to himself, "Desperate times call for desperate measures."

He hardly noticed the blood from his half nail-less finger. It dripped down the cell phone screen while he frantically dialed the one person who might be able to solve his problem. He didn't want to call him, and he didn't care for his methods.

But what option do I have? The stakes are just too high.

T-Minus 3 Years

Chapter 6 - Location: Silicon Valley, United States

Brent and Shayla's silicon valley home was located on the gradual, rocky slopes of the Mountain View terrace with a perfect view overlooking the lake. The rare hard rain had driven away any late-evening walkers ambling about with thoughts of acquisitions, taking their startups public, and the latest breakthroughs in technology that would surely change the world. The rain pounded down on the windows in hard sheets.

Ding-Dong!

The doorbell sounded, and the rain drowned out the sound as it carried lightly through the empty, decorated rooms of the house. In the living room, a thick layer of dust lay on neatly arranged artifacts: Shayla's doctorate degree, Brent's Fort Benning Combatives fighting championship trophy, their smiling faces in their framed wedding photo. This was Brent and Shayla's first house together, and it was full of good memories. There were a couple of extra bedrooms for the kids they planned to have. Here, they hosted many of the tech world's elite, the new space industry's luminaries, and many of the area's smartest and wealthiest. They devised their own world-changing ideas in this house, spending late nights working on their crazy plans and lazy Sunday mornings snuggling in bed. They had been living the dream.

Ding-Dong, Ding-Dong!

The rain came down even harder now, and the muffled sound of the doorbell died out as it carried through the halls, past the dining room and into the kitchen. Instead of dust, everything was covered with a thin film of filth. Dirty dishes overflowed from the sink. Pizza boxes were stacked high in the corner. Flies buzzed about the room, swarming over the trashcan, seeming to enjoy the permeating smell of mold and whiskey. At the kitchen island table a precarious stack of bills and mail spilled onto the floor and around a bowl of half-eaten Chinese food noodles takeout.

And there, Brent sat.

In his hand was a glass with another double's worth of whiskey. The bottle next to the glass was half-full.

"Ever the optimist, even till the end," Brent said to himself and laughed out loud, swatting too dumbly and slowly at the fly that chanced upon his arm.

The impatient doorbell sounded again and again, but Brent was too lost in thought to hear it. He finished off the rest of the whiskey in one gulp, face twisted and lips puckered. He'd never gotten used to that.

He opened the table drawer at his side and sifted through the contents with a detached certainty and a sigh. He turned back to the photo in the frame in front of him. Picking it up with both hands, he opened his mouth to speak.

BANG. BANG. BANG.

Brent dropped the frame and jumped to his feet, looking around, feeling guilty and exposed like a deer in headlights. Someone was knocking at the back door, and hard.

BANG. BANG. BANG.

"Open up, Brent!" came a muffled voice. "I know you're in there!"

"Crap!" said Brent.

He bent quickly and pulled the plastic tarp off the floor and grabbed the other section of tarp off the counter, balling them up as he walked to the back door. At the back door, the banging came again.

"Alright, coming!" Brent shouted, and sent the ball of plastic tarp sailing into the next room and over the side of the couch, out of sight.

BANG. BANG. BANG.

"You son of a bitch!" Brent shouted as he rushed to the door. "Now I'm gonna kick your..." Brent swung the door open to see Mike Johnson, the Chief Administrator of NASA, at his doorstep. "...Ass."

"You were saying?" said Johnson with eyebrow raised.

Johnson's nostrils expanded, probably taking in Brent's stink. Water from the hard rain poured off his fedora, through his exposed snow white hair, over the shoulders of his trench coat. He had a leather bound binder under his arm. Brent stared dumbfounded, mouth agape, hardly able to believe what his bloodshot eyes were seeing.

"Can I come in?" asked Johnson.

"Uh," said Brent. "Uh, no. You can't."

"Good," said Johnson, and he pushed past Carlson.

Brent shook his head as he followed Johnson into his kitchen. "And to what do I owe the pleasure, Johnson?"

Johnson replied, "I flew in from DC to check in on some projects at Ames. Figured I'd pay you a visit since I was in the neighborhood. It's been too long."

Brent's mind raced. What could the deputy director of the CIA, turned Top Chief at NASA want with me now?

"Are you drunk?" asked Johnson. "No matter. I'm here to see if you have any interest in finishing what you started."

Brent's eyebrows arched. "Don't screw with me, Johnson."

"Not screwing with you. You seem to be doing a good enough job screwing yourself up." He paused to give a disapproving shake of his head, then added, "The Mars Journey program is a go." You're the first civilian we've reached out to."

"Great, good luck *actually* pulling it off," said Brent dismissively. "As you said, I'm a bit screwed up right now. So why bother reaching out to me?"

"Besides you being a world class genius with a super computer brain?" asked Johnson. "Or are you forgetting that you led our research into prolonged space flight that led directly to planning for our Mars missions?"

"I've heard all this before."

"But have you heard the latest news?" asked Johnson. "As one of the most recognizable astronauts on the planet, the global Mars Now reality show contest has you ranked at number one in their latest poll."

"Wait, are you seriously planning on teaming up with them for the trip to Mars?"

"Oh yeah. The top three contestants after you are those kids from Japan, India, and Brazil."

"Kids? Space is no place for kids!"

"Well technically they're all over eighteen, but—"

Brent threw up his hands and turned to walk away. "I don't care about kids or contests! I just want you to—"

"Brent," said Johnson, taking a serious tone. "You're one of the primary architects of the Journey program. One ship sent to orbit Mars. That's two years in the cold of space with a crew of 12 to include the Mars Now contestants, an American Astronaut, a Russian Cosmonaut, a European Civilian, and—of all things—a Chinese Taikonaut. That's an insanely high level of risk, and all their lives are at stake."

"And money is at stake too right? It's always about the money with you."

"Of course it's always about the money. But that's not the point, because thanks to you, this mission is happening on an accelerated schedule. After you and your wife made that speech at the UN—"

"And my wife is dead now because of that speech!" snapped Brent.

Brent's words echoed through the kitchen.

Johnson closed his eyes and inhaled deeply.

"So forgive me if I don't share your bold enthusiasm." Brent crossed the kitchen to the table to grab for his bottle of whiskey.

"Come on, Brent." Johnson returned. "We've been over this before. It was a freak accident."

"A freak accident? Her car crashed over the side of a highway bridge with no witnesses. That's not a little suspect?"

Johnson said nothing.

"Her last text to me said she was approached by a strange man in the parking lot of the NewSpace launch complex."

"I told you we followed up on that lead. It was simply an overzealous fan of hers."

"Right, just a fan. You have an answer for everything..." Brent's words trailed off. "I couldn't even say goodbye to her, Mike. They never found her body. How do you explain that?"

"The river's current was too strong—."

"I don't want to hear any more of your excuses! My wife was murdered," Brent yelled, spittle flying, "and it was Herr Graden! I just know it!"

Brent slammed his fist down on the table punctuating his last point. His hand caught the edge of the takeout container and noodles flew in the air, catching him in the face before they slopped to the ground.

"Wow..." said Johnson. "Just, wow. Looks like I *did* come to the wrong place. First off, I called in more favors on this one with my CIA and intelligence *friends* than you can count. Nothing was found."

Brent hadn't even bothered to wipe his face.

"And you're lucky Herr Graden was gracious enough not to sue you for slander with your unfounded outburst to the press."

"Unfounded? I conducted my own investigation—"

"And regardless of that," continued Johnson, "Shayla would be ashamed to see you like this... And she would want you to finish what you started."

"Don't tell me what Shayla would want!" Brent lunged at Johnson but slipped on the spilled noodles and crashed to the floor in a heap.

Johnson shook his head again. "Look, I always had a soft spot for you. Despite your *smart mouth*, you have a good heart. I'm sorry to see you like this. But more importantly, I'm sorry I came by."

Johnson turned to leave. Brent, still on the ground, asked, "Are they really going with the international mission? China too?"

"Yes."

"That's exactly what she... What we wanted."

"Well, this mission is happening," said Johnson. "And you're in no shape to help. Do yourself a favor. Clean yourself up. Now if you'll excuse me, I've got some jet setting to take care of. And let's just say my hemorrhoids aren't going to like sitting on an eighteen-hour flight to Paris."

Johnson made his way to the door.

"Johnson!" Brent called.

Johnson turned. "Yeah?"

"Have fun in Paris," said Brent. "By the way, do you go around telling everybody about your hemorrhoids like that? Cause that is really just TMI."

Johnson laughed. "There's a glimmer of the Brent I know." He started to leave again.

"Wait," Brent said as he stood, noodles dropping from him as he rose. "Why the hell did you come here in the first place?"

"Oh, to drop this off," Johnson said, unzipping and reaching into his binder. "A ticket to fly with me to Paris, and then China, and then to Russia, to recruit the crew of the Journey. But you don't look up to it." He dropped the ticket on the counter next to the door. "And maybe you should think about cutting that long hair, hippie."

"Not a chance," Brent said with a forced smile as the door closed.

He was all alone now, and the only sound came from the driving rain. Brent wiped tears from his eyes with back of his hands as he picked up the ticket. He walked back to the table with ticket in hand and looked down at the photo of Shayla.

"I don't know if I can do this without you," said Brent. "I don't know if I have it in me for one last trip around the world."

Chapter 7

Johnson stood at the priority boarding lane at the airport. It was early in the morning. He was used to early mornings. He glanced down the terminal, saw no sign of what he was looking for, and shook his head.

"Now boarding first class," came the announcement.

"Oh, well," Johnson said, letting out with a sigh as he queued in the priority boarding lane.

"Johnson!" he suddenly heard. Out of the corner of his eye, he spotted someone running through the terminal. Johnson didn't turn. He just kept his eyes down on his ticket.

"Johnson!" said the voice, coming up from behind him. "Come on now, I know you hear me."

"Looks like you made it," said Johnson, still not looking at Brent.

"Yeah," said Brent. "I guess so. But I'm sure you knew I would."

"Me?" said Johnson as the attendant scanned his ticket. "Nah, don't know what you're talking about."

Brent had his ticket scanned next.

"I'm sorry, sir," said the attendant. "You have to board in Zone 5."

Brent looked quizzically at Johnson. "Zone 5? Really?"

"What?" said Johnson. "You expect us to buy a first-class ticket for a most likely chance of no show? This is still the government after all. Heck, I even had to use my own airline points to upgrade."

"Great. Guess I'll see you on there in thirty minutes."

"That will give me plenty of time to tell the stewardesses not to serve you any alcohol."

"Well, that's just great," Johnson heard Brent say, as he stepped around the corner onto the loading ramp. "Now this is going to be one long flight."

Part 2 - Recruit the Crew

Chapter 8 - Location: Paris, France

By the time Brent made it to the European Space Agency headquarters, situated in the heart of Paris, Sebastian Schmidt, the Administrator for the European Space Agency, had been at the podium for quite some time. Brent quickly took a place next to Johnson.

"Can't believe this place is located directly in the middle of the city," Brent whispered to Johnson. "Traffic was horrible."

"What's horrible is you didn't pack a suit," replied Johnson. "You would have been just fine if you hadn't had to stop off and buy one."

Brent responded with a shrug.

"Today is a great day," said the administrator. "Dr. Andrea Martine, in partnership with Herr Graden and GradenTech industries, will be going to Mars as part of the Mars Journey Program. Her secondary backup is the British astronaut Keith Davies. Let's give them a round of applause."

The packed room gave a lengthy standing ovation. Brent was still reeling from the GradenTech partnership announcement when he realized he was the only one not standing. He stood and joined in. He looked over to Andrea standing close by, and their eyes met briefly. She looked away before he could say anything.

After the clapping died down and everyone regained their seats, Schmidt continued. "Andrea is no stranger to space. She was a pioneer in the Commercial Space Productivity and Exploration program, and has been to space on three separate occasions. Andrea, please come say some words and answer some questions."

Andrea approached the mic amidst applause. Her short hair was now a darker shade of red, and even though Brent had worked with her a few times since the rescue mission on the doomed *Pisces*, he was still taken aback at the contrast in Andrea from before. On the many research videos and news clips that Brent watched on long nights asking too many "what if?" questions, Andrea pre-*Pisces* seemed an upbeat idealist. this version of Andrea taking the mic, seemed to be all cold hearted business.

"Thank you all so much. For those who were present, you'll surely know that Administrator Schmidt covered a great deal of mission information earlier." Her eyes subtly glanced over to where Brent was seated. "Suffice it to say I am very excited for this opportunity. I have dreamed of going to Mars ever since I was a girl. All of my research has been preparation for this trip. Please, do you have any questions?" she asked.

A reporter from Channel Une News spoke up. "Why do you think, with all of the poor and homeless and hungry people in France, we should be dedicating our precious money to space travel?"

"We will always have poverty," said Andrea. "We will always have hungry people. That is a sad state of affairs, but it is the truth. And will remain so until we have technology to treat their mental conditions quickly and cheaply, technology that can provide low-cost, nonperishable, high-density nutrition, and we are working on just such programs with our new partnership with Gradentech on the Mars Journey Mission. We can sit back and watch others suffer and wonder why, or we can get off our asses, take on major challenges, and let those less fortunate bask in the benefits of such accomplishments."

"That may explain poverty, but what about government spending?" said a journalist from PNN News. "That's through the roof. After bailing out many nations, there are some who think we are at the end ourselves?"

"Do you know how many great civilizations have died?" said Andrea. "How many great extinctions have occurred throughout the course of history? We are in the middle of a runaway, man-made extinction. We are in the middle of a collapse of society as we know it. One of the hallmarks of fallen civilizations is that they have done nothing to stop it until it's too late. Here's the thing. You can't think yourself out of the hole. You have to climb. Only through great works can we achieve great results. We are at risk of blowing ourselves up, of warring with our neighbors over oil and water and honor. In order to get past that, we need to get past this petty race for yesterday's scraps, and get busy working on technology that will usher in tomorrow's abundance."

The reporters stared with their mouths agape in the face of Andrea's fierce proclamations.

"And don't even get me started on the risk of an asteroid strike," she continued. "Jesus. We can spend billions of dollars bailing out a fiscally irresponsible nation that doesn't want to work hard or be financially intelligent, but to propose that same amount to ensure the survival of our species is actually up for debate? Really? That's all the questions I'll be taking, for now. You can find any other answers in my new book that just launched today, *The Mars Ultimatum*. I'm sure Keith Davies has many things to say to you. Au revoir!"

Cameras flashed and reporters surged as Andrea walked off to the side of the stage toward the stairs. Brent cut off her path and stood there clapping overdramatically. "I wanted to say congratulations. Well done, and well deserved."

"Oh, so very good to see you too," Andrea said. "Well, how did you like that?"

Not wasting further words or sarcastic gestures, Brent stepped forward and said, "What are you thinking? When you make a deal with Herr Graden, you make a deal with the devil. Remember that the devil always comes out on top."

"And working with Ken Solum is any different?" said Andrea. "Solum and his New Space Enterprises are the ones funding your little trip around the world, and you had no problem taking both Solum's and Graden's money to support our earlier joint research projects like the Unified Mars Path Papers. And let's not forget their money was all over you and your wife's endeavors..."

Brent arched his eyebrows.

"Oh" said Andrea. "I'm so sorry, Brent. I didn't mean to bring her up. It took me such a long time to get over Jean Louis..."

"Yes, there is a difference," interrupted Brent before the feelings of guilt that rose up in his stomach could stop his momentum. "The difference is intent. It's the difference of knowing what one is trying to do."

"Fine, if that's how you want to be. Just don't confuse yourself. When you start trying to figure out men like Solum and Graden you have no ground to stand on. It's not worth your time."

"That shouldn't stop you from trying to figure it out."

"Such a charming man as usual," said Andrea. "I really must be going. I have a trip to Mars to plan for. Enjoy the city. We have some of the finest wine in the world. I read you are partial to drink as of late, no?"

"Wait, where did you read that?"

Andrea just gave a snide look in reply as she walked off, though Brent thought he caught a glimpse of her expression turn to worry as she headed for the stairs.

Well that woman hasn't changed a bit! He stepped out on to the streets of Paris, his eyes scanning the streets, the neat, white façades of the architecture. His eyes drifted to the signs in the cafés.

Vin, bière, aperitif... thought Brent. You know what, I'm actually feeling like I'll just have a coffee. Shows what she knows.

Brent started to take a step forward when he felt the tug of something on his shirt. He turned to look behind him, saw no one, then looked down into the upturned, smiling face of a kid with a rocket ship in one hand and a smartphone in the other. He was probably twelve years old and wore a "Mars or Bust" t-shirt.

"Monsieur, are you an astronaut?" said the kid.

Brent crinkled his nose and raised his voice a little. "Do I look like an astronaut?"

The boy averted his eyes. "No... but my dad said you were one of the best."

Brent looked past the boy. Nearby stood a man, presumably his father, also wearing a "Mars or Bust" shirt.

"I didn't believe him, though," added the kid as he turned to walk away.

"Wait..." said Brent. "Your dad is partially correct. I *was* an astronaut."

The boy turned back, excited. "Really?! I'm going to be an astronaut, someday. I'm going to live on Mars!"

Brent couldn't help but laugh. "Really, now? And why is that?"

"Because it's cool! And it gets me excited, and it will be great to look back to Earth from another planet and wave to my friends and family."

"Because it's cool," said Brent. "That's a perfectly fine reason."

"But when I tell the kids at school, they just laugh at me and say I'm too short."

Brent ducked down to the boy's level. "Really? Too short? That shouldn't be a problem. Regulation suits accommodate persons as short as 1.5 meters. As a matter of fact, being smaller has its advantages in tight quarters of space."

"Really?" said the boy, lighting up.

"Oh, yes," said Brent. "Want to know the secret to becoming an astronaut?"

"Hell yeah!" The boy covered his mouth and looked back at his dad. "I mean, yes, sir."

Brent laughed again but quickly regained his sincere demeanor. "You have to want it more than anything. You have to believe in it more than anything. You have to start training right now. You have to do really good in sports, and you have to do really good in school. You have to be productive and kind, and volunteer, and do interesting and exciting things."

"So, you're basically saying I have to be a good person in order to be an astronaut?"

"Hmm. Yeah... I guess, in a way, I am. Wanting to be an astronaut, to go out to the farthest reaches of human exploration, requires you to be the best of humanity."

"I don't know if I can do that. It sounds like hard work."

"Well, it is hard work... But it's also one of the most natural things in the world, if you want it bad enough. And I think you will be an excellent astronaut."

"Really?"

"Oh yeah. One of the best. What's your name?"

"Jacques," said the boy. "Jacques Toussaint." He snapped to attention and saluted with the rocket ship still in his hand.

"Excellent," said Brent, laughing.

Jacques's face turned quizzical. He looked up into Brent's eyes. "So, if to be an astronaut you have to be a good person, are you no longer an astronaut because you aren't a good person?"

Brent felt as though a donkey had kicked him in the stomach. He hadn't been expecting that question, and he didn't like the resounding answer that filled his mind.

"Are you alright, monsieur?" asked Jacques.

"Yeah," said Brent. "Say, you want to get a picture with me and your dad?"

"Sure!"

Jacques's father walked over and as they posed for a group selfie, Brent felt like he had never wanted a drink more in his life.

Chapter 9

Andrea entered her office with a feeling of dread sinking into her stomach. Reluctantly, she set up a video conference call with the GradenTech COO, Vanessa Dorn. Dorn answered with a strained look on her face.

"Graden would like to speak with you," she said. "Personally."

"Wait, why?" stammered Andrea, but Dorn disappeared and the screen went black.

Why are you acting like a scared little girl? Steel your nerves, Andrea mentally reassured herself.

"That was a very effective press conference," said Graden unexpectedly, the screen still dark. His voice had a very slight electronic quality to it. Andrea thought for a second that it was a bad connection, but she remembered reading Graden had sustained a throat injury as a child making it difficult to speak. He created an advanced cybernetic implant to overcome his limitation, and then made billions licensing the technology.

"Thank you," she said swallowing. "I hope it had the effect you were looking for."

"It did. However, I was not expecting you to promote your book launch. Last I heard, that wasn't for many months."

"Well, I figured I'd take advantage of the occasion."

"I don't like deviations from the plan, especially without being informed."

"Now look, I only agreed to this partnership for the resources to get to Mars, not because I wanted someone watching over my shoulder—"

"The reasons you agreed to the partnership are inconsequential," said Graden, cutting her off. "The relevant fact is that you agreed. As did I. We are contributing considerable sums. And the nature of this venture requires a bit of over-the-shoulder watching, as you say... You should normalize yourself to that aspect quickly."

"And why are you contributing so much?"

"Once again," said Graden, "the why is inconsequential. What does bear consequences is if anyone in the partnership decides not to honor their side of the agreement, which is not something that would be taken lightly."

"Of course," said Andrea. "I am nothing if not a business-minded woman. To Mars, then. Thank you for the assistance, it will really—"

"That will be all," interrupted Graden, and then the connection went dead.

"Be helpful..." said Andrea, letting the words trail off.

As Graden cut out, Andrea found herself thinking back to the words of Brent Carlson, and she wondered, *What the hell kind of deal with the devil did I make?*

Chapter 10 - Location: Beijing, China

The flight from Paris to Beijing was long. It's way more comfortable strapped in an advanced space capsule then it is flying economy for 12 hours, thought Brent.

The thing that amazed him the most about China was the sheer number of people there. The airport and streets were so crowded. Like New York City on steroids. But the scene that was laid out before him at the Mars Journey Program Taikonauts recruitment ceremony was unlike anything he had ever seen.

A virtual sea of people swarmed and swirled, focused intently on the stage like spectators at a massive festival rock concert. Chinese National Space Agency security detail estimated the participants at over 100,000. They'd been waiting all day for the main act. Rockets were featured prominently to the left and right of the stage, dominating the view and displaying the evolution of this proud nation's space exploration history.

The crowd was charged with anticipation, surging back and forth with the sound of national songs being broadcast. Hard to know how anybody could see the stage from the back, but that wasn't important. What was important was that they were here to demonstrate their pride and to be present when the announcement was made. The announcement that China was going to Mars.

They filed out onto the stage. Dignitary after dignitary. Some of China's greatest leaders, ambassador Jiang, some delegates from America, NASA Administrator Johnson, and Ming Han, the country's greatest taikonaut. This was good company to be in.

The crowd soared and surged at the mere glimpse of Han. He was their nation's finest, best, and brightest. Marching out behind him, seemingly unnoticed by the crowd, was Ling Li.

Brent noticed the contrast in reaction from Han to Li. That was the difference between being number one and number two. Li was probably one of top 100 most qualified individuals on the planet to fly to Mars, but that didn't matter in the eyes of the people. They only cared about the best.

Tough break, kid, Brent thought to himself, as he made his way to the row of seats at the back of the stage.

Li had been to space, aced all his tests. He was an avid watcher and reader of western books and movies. That sometimes got him in trouble. Everyone did it, but Li did it more than others. What was more amazing was his ability to deal with the culture over a long period of time, which was one of the reasons he'd been selected.

China was sending their best two taikonauts for the two-year training mission. Only one would actually get to go on the fourteen-month Mars journey, the first ever human flyby of the red planet, followed by fame and glory, as the first speaker at the podium was now saying to the enormous crowd.

Ambassador Jiang gave a speech. Fortitude. Cooperation.

Blah, blah, blah, thought Brent.

Not that he disagreed with it. It was just you could only hear the same catchphrases and clichés so many times. Well, in this case, he was reading the English translation that the monitors were broadcasting towards the English-speaking delegates.

Now, NASA Administrator Johnson was up. Unity. Exploration. Brent actually had heard this speech word-for-word before. It was translated by an interpreter.

Next up was Han. Brent had never met the man, but his reputation was legendary across the members of the elite group of men and women who had the job of going to space. His stamina was off the charts. He seemingly didn't need to sleep on long missions, and had the mind and dexterity of a hi-speed factory floor sorting machine. If Li was top one hundred in the world, Han was top five, maybe even number one, as many of his fellow astronauts ranked him. The existence of such rankings were a closely guarded secret, of course.

Brent watched Han approach the mic. The entire crowd quieted. Dignitaries watched awestruck. The crowd looked on in anticipation, and Han began. From the crowd's reaction Brent could tell it was a rousing speech. A damn good speech. The interpreter screen kept showing the key points. Honor. Pride. Sacrifice. Excellence.

Brent looked to his left to where Li was sitting. Li's face dropped. His mouth hung open like a comic book character. He kept mouthing the words, "No, no, no."

Brent bumped him with his elbow, and whispered sharply, "Hey, you alright?"

Li just turned to Brent and said, "No. No, I am not. That's... my speech."

The crowd roared to life, and the sound was deafening. Han raised his hand and waved to the crowd and made his way back to the chairs without addressing anyone.

Is that a grin on his face? thought Brent.

"And now, presenting, Ling Li," said the announcer in Chinese.

Li stood slowly. The crowd went from high decibel to quiet enough to hear a pin drop.

Li adjusted the microphone, and it squealed with feedback.

"Well, how do I follow that, right?" said Li with a nervous chuckle.

The crowd's reaction was muted, not a sound.

"Well, Han covered a lot of what I was gonna say, and if I didn't know any better, I'd say he copied my speech."

The crowd responded with some murmurs.

"Well, I mean seriously, almost word for word. It was good speech though, right?"

The crowd began to boo.

The kid is bombing and choking all at once, thought Brent. This just got interesting.

"I'm kidding, I'm just kidding," Li responded desperately.

Now, a louder chorus of boos.

"Really?" said Li in English, squinting out at the crowd. "Who's booing me? Who is doing that?"

Just when the crowd was about to unleash their displeasure, Han appeared at Li's side and took the mic.

"Taikonaut Li may not have the social graces of an elite world leader," Han said to the crowd, "or the wisdom of an experienced sage."

The crowd was quiet and curious now. Li, who was staring a hole into the side Han's head, whispered under his breath, "Where are you going with this?"

"I can attest that Li does have the heart of a warrior," said Han to some cheers from the crowd. "I can personally vouch that Li does have the discipline of a champion taikonaut."

The crowd grew louder as Han whipped them up into a frenzy.

"And I have no doubt that if called to, Li will lay his life on the line to advance our great nation."

At this, the crowd roared. Han grabbed Li's hand and raised it, and the crowd roared louder. Li couldn't help but let a smile wash over his face. Li walked off to their seats with Han's arm around his shoulder.

"Thanks for the save," said Li.

"Thanks for the speech notes," said Han.

"You sonnofa—"

"You shouldn't leave them lying around," Han said, cutting him off.

They hugged and laughed louder than before, and that was the end of the ceremony. The crowd was being told that they were the people of the future.

The dignitaries rose to their feet as the crowd was told to begin dispersing peacefully and in disciplined fashion. Han and Li shook hands with the Chinese leaders and ambassadors, Jiang, and Johnson.

When Han got around to shake Carlson's hand, he just looked down at it, then back at Carlson, and said in Chinese, "You disgraced the greatest role a man can play on this planet. I don't even know why they let you stand here amongst us."

Brent, sensing the anger in his words, said, "So no hand shake then?"

Han looked him in the eyes and said in English, "You don't look so good. I don't want to catch whatever you have." Then, he turned and marched off the stage.

Li stepped in and shook Brent's hand, saying, "Pleased to meet you."

"Great to meet you, as well," said Brent. "You wouldn't happen to know what all that was about, would you?"

"Han is just a very honorable person," said Li, "and he may feel that your actions were less than honorable."

"I see. And do you feel my actions were less than honorable?"

"Hard to say. You pretty much denigrated your entire chain of command, from the bottom up to the president, and everywhere in between. You lashed out at the entire astronaut corps for not having your back, and then leveled horrible allegations of murder and deceit at the titans of industry who create the hardware and systems that got you to space."

"When you put it that way," said Brent, "it doesn't sound that good."

"But..." said Li. "You might be right, and if you're right about all that, and everyone is wrong, that means you are the most honorable of all, because you are willing to do and say what no one else will."

"Holy crap, you certainly put a lot of thought into this."

"Well, the answer to your question is simple. I don't know if you were less than honorable, and I have no way of telling, so I choose to take the best of what you have to offer and ignore the rest. And what you have to offer in regards to Mars travel is extraordinary."

"How do you know all this?"

"From you and your wife's book, the Unified Mars Path Papers, and other sources..."

Brent raised his eyebrows at that. "I'm not sure I like the sound of *other sources*."

"Look," said Li. "In your Mars Fitness study papers, you postulate that Greco-Roman wrestling, Brazilian jujitsu, and submission grappling in general may be the best sports to be taken up in preparation for long-term flights in space."

"Correct," said Brent. "These forms of exercise, as long as they are performed with discipline and safety in mind, should be the best exercises to maintain muscle mass, bone density, and cardiovascular capacity. The additional point is that these activities can be fun, and taken on as a group activity, they rank above any other."

"Precisely! However, I've been thinking that you may have introduced a bias into your hypothesis. Since you are an expert in these areas, as well as qigong, you are drawn to them and understand them better."

"That's a good point, but you have to start with what you have, and bias seeps into almost everything. There is very rarely pure, unbiased science anywhere."

"That is why I plan on starting with what I know. I am a lifelong master of wushu, and a high level traditional kung fu practitioner. I believe that our training methods will be able to generate muscle mass and bone density retention with less risk of injury than submission grappling over a long duration space flight."

"There's only really one way to test that," said Brent. "And that's on the trip to Mars. And unfortunately, neither myself, nor most likely you, are going to get to test that. And wait a minute, how do you know I studied qigong? I only started training that after the Mars Fitness paper."

"Well..." said Li, scratching sheepishly at the back of his head. "There are quite a few fan websites set up that track your day-to-day activities."

Brent recovered from being momentarily stunned, "And you think it's okay to spy on me?"

"I'm not the one that's actually doing the spying... and I don't really read those for very long anyway, I just get the info I need and get out."

"Well that's good you don't read them very long. I guess they also list what I eat, and what my favorite drinks are."

"Lo mein and whiskey."

Brent stared with a look of horror and disgust. "I'm not too thrilled at the idea of having my entire life dissected. And I guess Han was right, I'm not feeling too well." At that, Brent turned heel, and walked hurriedly towards the stage exit.

"Wait! I had another question!" Li called after Brent.

"Why don't you just Google it? I'm sure someone out there has already figured out my answer on the matter."

As Brent left the stage, he barely made out Li's parting words "Wow, what happened to that guy?"

Chapter 11

The sun was setting, and Li was kicking, punching, and sweating hard. He was in the third of five rows, each made up of twenty taikonauts, one hundred taikonauts en masse for martial arts training in the open air Chinese National Space Agency Sports Training Facility. Each of the taikonauts moved flawlessly in step with one another and in synchrony with the rhythm of the count, following the wushu instructor at the head of the rows. It didn't matter that Li or Han were the top picks for the Mars Journey program. When it came to training, they were the same as everyone else.

Sweat dropped into Li's eyes and stung. It didn't matter. All that mattered was execution of the moves, in time, exactly at the right time. The instructor was too far away for him to really be followed, therefore, each practitioner had to memorize 100 steps for this Taolu, or form as the westerners called them. Each form would flow into the next. There were ten master forms designed to keep discipline as part of the basics of the corps. Taikonauts didn't get time in class to practice, so they practiced on their own time. Memorize these 1000 steps, practice them daily, and you rewired your brain and body to quickly memorize activities that would take days for most astronauts to memorize.

A culture of discipline is just one of the reasons the Chinese are such a logical choice for space cooperation, Li thought. He realized he was breaking his concentration, and refocused on the moves.

The second part of the equation was the iron will of China. China had made space travel and travel to Mars a top priority in their 100-year plan. *Nothing would stop them, and so it made sense for other nations to team up rather than try to race against them.*

Li entered into a particularly challenging sequence of jumps, kicks, and whirlwind arm patterns. From a bird's -eye view, it must have looked like magic. Li grinned, caught himself, and returned to neutral look.

The third and most potent part of the cooperation equation is China's massive wealth, Li thought as they all began the ninth form for the day. Two to go.

China bought the best technology available. They hired and trained the best scientists and engineers. Problems that would take years to solve took less time because they would just integrate more people. And then there was the fact that China's wealthy citizens gave freely to nonprofit projects that aligned with China's goals to show their loyalty to the republic and gain popularity. Since Li's father was a managing director of the world's largest electronics manufacturing conglomerate, TechShareZ, and since he had donated large sums of money to space program projects, there was rampant speculation that was the reason Li had been selected for the Mars Journey Program over so many others.

That just isn't right, Li thought, his anger rising as they transitioned into the final form. I worked my butt off. I trained my butt off. I earned my place. I've always fought for what I had. I don't care what any of them say.

Li began to realize that he no longer heard the lead instructor calling out moves. He began to look up at those who surrounded him and realized they had stopped. All of their eyes were on him, and then it dawned on him that he had begun the wrong form sequence. They had started a new one the day before. Lost in his thoughts, he had erred. Li stopped and bowed to the instructor.

The instructor said, "Seems the prospect of training with the Americans has already started to affect your discipline."

"No, Shifu!" Shouted Li, with his eyes lowered.

"Ah, so then, you think you are better then everyone now because you have been selected, is that it?" queried the instructor.

"No, Shifu!" replied Li again, his voice sounding more dejected, his eyes looking even lower to the ground.

"Then enlighten us."

"I lost focus while thinking about the great glory we will bring our nation, Shifu."

"You will bring us only shame if you behave in this manner. You will bring us only death. It is not your purpose to wonder and gloat and be in awe. It is your purpose to execute and act out the will of your nation."

"Yes, Shifu."

"Now, it is your purpose to sit up here facing the class, drink some water, and relax as your fellow taikonauts start the form over again from the first."

No sound was made from the individuals in the platoon, but Li could feel their hatred burning at him through their eyes.

"Shifu, I would like to..."

"Do not shame yourself a second time!"

"Yes, Shifu!" Li shouted as he ran to the front, picked up a water bottle, and sat down facing the group.

"Besides," the instructor continued, "you should be used to the rich and relaxed existence."

At this, the crowd let out a laugh, and Li's face burned with embarrassment and infuriation.

As luck would have it, Han was in the front row directly in front of Li. Han never looked at Li for the entire ten forms. His discipline was strong. His disappointment for Li was even stronger. Li could feel it, and he vowed to never make a mistake like that again.

Chapter 12 - Location: Star City, Near Moscow, Russia

Cigar smoke and the smell of vodka filled the confines of the tiny conference room at the Russian Federal Space Agency Headquarters. *This decor literally looks like it's been around since the 70s, 60s—maybe even the 50s,* thought Brent. The room was cramped, hot, and loud. There were liters of 80 proof vodka sitting right in front of Brent, and drinking it or not drinking it was the least of his worries. Brent had a bad feeling about where all of this was heading.

The ride from the airport had been pretty straightforward. A twelve-hour flight from Beijing, followed by a two-hour ride here to Russia's Space Administration. Johnson had told him along the way that there were two parts to today's mission: recruitment, and then a special surprise. Brent didn't like surprises, not in space, not on trips to Russia. Especially not on trips to Russia.

The man to his left wore a business suit that looked the same age as the conference room. He had a cigar in one hand and a drink in the other, and he kept offering Brent the bottle. As a matter of fact, it was impolite and rude to refuse. Brent's resistance wearing down, he looked up across the table to see the cold hard stare of Administrator Johnson.

He turned to his comrade to his left, and spoke in Russian. He had picked up a bit from his time on the ISS.

"Regrettably, I must decline," he said. "My stomach is feeling ill".

"Bah! This will make your stomach feel better," said the man, slapping Brent on the back. He started to pour a glass but stopped when the main doors opened to reveal the Russian Administrator of space, Vadim Kuznetsov. Everyone at the table shut up and stood, and Brent followed suit.

Kuznetsov was followed by Yuri Danko and Natasha Predurnska. Yuri was the nation's most well-known cosmonaut and the most experienced. His bright blonde buzz cut and tall lanky frame set him apart from the majority of the corps. He held the world record for the most time in space, and now in his late-forties, he was approaching the end of his career. What a great final mission, to fly by the planet Mars.

Natasha was the number two pick, and though not as experienced, she represented the new breed of Russian cosmonauts.

Yuri stood to Brent's right, and Administrator Kuznetsov moved to stand beside Johnson.

"Good to see you again," said Johnson.

"Indeed, it is," said Kuznetsov. "We caught you on the news in China, making quite a proceeding of the recruitment of Han. China is a great friend of Russia, but they are still relatively new to this game of space, so it is understandable that they would flex their might and make a big show of the event. Hope you'll forgive us if we're not as given to... excessive celebration and ceremony."

"No forgiveness needed," said Johnson. "We've both been in the *space game*, as you call it, for quite some time. Now, while space travel is rather routine—"

"Especially now that you have your own manned launch capabilities again," interjected Kuznetsov, a bit tongue-in-cheek.

"Of course," said Johnson, "but I would say we grew closer for the arrangement while it lasted, wouldn't you? Now that we have our own launch capabilities again, space travel is a bit routine. But you and I can hopefully agree that this journey to Mars is anything but."

"Yes, yes, of course," Kuznetsov said. "And officially, for the sake of minor ceremony and posterity, we formally accept the roles of number one and number two Russian cosmonauts as part of the program. Though we all have worked together to form the program, we will rely on the Americans as the primary program managers, if you will. Though any glory and accolades will go to the group of nations present for the flyby. And the honor will go to the human race as we continue on our forward course of progress."

Johnson had a big smile on his face. "We're more than happy to share that glory with the people of this world, as you say, Administrator."

"Of course, since you have won out the day as primary program managers," said Kuznetsov, "anything that goes wrong with the program—and most assuredly it will not, but if it did—would fall back into your lap. I'm sure you are well aware, yes?"

Johnson smiled even bigger now. "We're pretty used to taking on the bulk of the work and responsibility for big challenges. This will be no different. Glad we are in agreement. Shall we shake on that?"

"Shake? I'll do you one better, here behind closed doors and away from the cameras. We'll drink to that!"

The room laughed and cheered. Glasses were filled and vodka passed around. The glass in front of Brent was filled.

"To our united journey," said Administrator Kuznetsov, and he raised his glass. Everyone raised their glasses. "Let us drink to the success of our project."

Everyone drank. Brent quickly dumped his vodka and pretended to take a shot, not wanting to catch the attention of the man to his left. Instead, he caught the attention of Yuri, who looked down at where the vodka had landed.

"You know, we will charge you for the cleanup of that," said Yuri. "This floor has never had a drop of vodka spilled on it..."

Brent turned to face Yuri. "Well, you know what? From the looks of the clumsy people in here, I'd say that this floor has seen more than its fair share of vodka spills."

Yuri inched close to Brent's face. "You calling me a liar?"

Brent leaned in closer. His and Yuri's noses were almost touching. "I'm not just calling you a liar," said Brent. "I'm calling you a no-good yellow-bellied liar."

The room quieted and all eyes turned to them.

Yuri's eye twitched.

Brent's lip twitched.

"Draw!" shouted Yuri.

Brent and Yuri raised their hands up in mock guns and mock fired at one another. Laughing now, they hugged one another. The room, realizing this was just the game of two old friends who had spent almost a year together in space, went back to their conversations and drinks.

"It's been too long," said Brent.

"Indeed it has, old friend," said Yuri. "And you seem to have aged twenty years."

"Thanks, I appreciate that. So, you excited for this or what?"

"This is the mission. I was selected for it. I will be four years away from my family. My boys. Heck, odds are we won't even make it up there. But let's just say I have a job to do. And I will do it."

"Great outlook, pal," Brent said.

"Sorry you won't be going along for the ride, odds or no odds."

"Ah, you'll be fine. Besides, I couldn't stand another year with you in cramped quarters. It's your smell, really."

Yuri laughed. "Well, looks like here is where we are parting ways."

"Oh," said Brent as he turned to see Johnson signaling him over. "Take care, Yuri."

"Same to you, Brent." And as he walked away he said, "And by the way, I'm really impressed with you dumping that drink. I've read that you've been having issues with that lately."

Brent could only stare after him. *Not you too, Yuri! I've got to find who is writing all this stuff. And when I do...*

Brent approached both Administrators still shaking his head. "Pleasure to meet you, Administrator Kuznetsov."

"I'm sure it is, Mr. Carlson," said Kuznetsov. "Now, Administrator Johnson here has just barely convinced me that you have the clearance for the tour."

"The tour?" queried Brent.

"Oh, good. Glad that Johnson could keep that part of the bargain."

"Shall we away then?" said Johnson.

Four armed Russian soldiers emerged from behind the door, assault rifles at the ready.

Brent turned to Johnson. "So this was your big surprise? I knew I hated surprises for a reason."

"Calm down, Mr. Carlson," said Kuznetsov. "This is just the armed escort for the tour. If you will come right this way."

They boarded an elevator.

"We are heading down thirty stories below the earth," said Kuznetsov. "Back in the Cold War days, we built these massive underground hangars to perform our research, engineering, and construction with little fear of interruption, should there be a nuclear attack."

"Great," said Brent. "You know I don't mind going up in space or in an airplane, but heading practically into the Earth's core isn't really my idea of a good time. Does anyone want to fill me in on what's going on?"

The military men just kept staring ahead. Johnson and Kuznetsov exchanged glances. Kuznetsov nodded. Johnson stepped forward and raised up the binder he had been carrying. He flipped to a page and turned it, motioning for Brent to take a look.

"Does that look familiar to you?" said Johnson.

"Wait," said Brent. "This is part of our group's proposal for a multinational, multi-corporation vessel that can get us to Mars using the best of the technology from our varied nations and corporations."

"That's correct. Now turn to the next tab."

Brent turned the page to reveal a rough graphical design of just such a vessel. "Hey, that's not bad. Not exactly what I had in mind. Actually, she's kind of ugly."

Johnson laughed. "What were you expecting, the *Enterprise*? That's what you get when you match up tech from twenty-five nations. You get a mutt. Well, this mutt's name is the *Journey I*. You don't like her?"

"No, I love her," said Brent. "She's great! But how will we get it done in time? Something this ambitious..."

"The only way we would be able to get it done in time is if it were already started," said Johnson.

"I agree."

"And that's why we're here."

At that, the elevator bay doors opened with an accompanying pneumatic whir, revealing the cavernous space of the underground Hangar Bay 99. The room was so massive that it took Brent a moment to realize his eyes weren't being tricked by an optical illusion.

Hundreds of workers moved to and fro, some in orange body suits and others in biohazard suits. Like bees in a hive, they buzzed back and forth, but all centered around the queen of the nest, the centerpiece of the room, the nearly completed body of the *Journey I* spacecraft.

"My God," let out Brent. "I can't believe it."

"Believe it, Mr. Carlson," said Kuznetsov.

"You guys really can put something together when you put your minds to it."

"So, still think she's ugly?" asked Johnson.

Brent laughed, "Not at all!"

"As humorous as you may think this is," said Kuznetsov, "I hope you realize the gravity of the situation. This is the most ambitious project in human history. This is, in part, from funding from the astronaut's nations, as well as the countries that just wanted their designs to become a piece of the journey. All these parts, ideas, and technologies have existed for a while. It's just now that we've put them together in this configuration. Then, disassembling them in logical chunks and shipping them around the world for a massive launch schedule that will start next year."

"Oh, I appreciate it, sir," said Brent. "I am in awe of it. This might just be the best surprise of my life!"

"So happy to hear that," Kuznetsov said, hardly able to contain his distaste. "Now, if you don't mind, we will be ending the grandstanding and sightseeing tour, and we'll be sending you away, as we must return to the actual business of space exploration."

"Can I get just fifteen minutes more to look around?" said Brent. "Can I?"

Kuznetsov looked over to Johnson and said in exasperation, "Can I actually tell our guest no?"

"You can try," said Johnson. "I haven't had much luck in my ten years knowing him."

"Very well," said Kuznetsov. "Fifteen minutes more."

Brent practically sprinted over to the *Journey I* spacecraft.

Chapter 13

Later that evening, Yuri parked his black, government issue SUV in front of his house located on the space administration compound. He got out slowly, knowing what he was most likely going to face when he got inside the house.

Scratch that, make it before I get in the house, thought Yuri, seeing his wife, Irina, already standing on the outside steps waiting for him.

"So, I assume you saw the news?" said Yuri.

"No," said Irina, "but my phone has been ringing off the hook with friends and family who did. Why didn't you tell me?"

"I didn't want you to worry."

"And what am I doing now?" she said. "You've been gone for so long, and now you'll be gone again for what? Three more years?"

"Four," said Yuri. "Four years. But you can visit, and we'll have web cam technology on the vessel."

"Web cam technology? That's how our children will get to see their father as they grow up?"

From behind Irina, the sound of a mini stampede was rising, and then three young boys with blond hair came bursting through the door.

"Papa!" they shouted in unison as they jumped into his arms and gripped up at him.

Looking back at his mother, one of the kids said, "Why are you crying, Mama?"

"Because Daddy is going to Mars," said Yuri, "and she is so happy for me. Isn't that right Mama?" He looked into her eyes with love, knowing she didn't want to upset the kids.

"Yes, of course," she said. "I am so happy. You should be so proud of your papa."

"Yay!" they shouted.

"Mars is so far away! Can we go?" one of his little ones asked.

"You can't come with me, but you know what you can do? You can get ice cream! Who wants ice cream?"

"Me, me, me!"

"Then go get your little butts in the truck. Go on, get in there."

They raced to the SUV, leaving Yuri and his wife alone.

"They love you so much, Yuri bear."

"I love them. And I love you. You know that, right?"

"Yes," she said, tears rolling down her face. "I know that, and I love you. I know you have to do this. And I will make sure you have everything you need."

"Oh? From the sound of that, we might just have a fourth on the way."

"Yuri!"

Yuri laughed, moved in, and kissed her, grabbing her ample body in his arms.

"Eww!" he heard from behind, the kids voicing their disapproval.

"Oh, you are going to get it!" Yuri mock yelled at them.

The kids all ducked under the windows in the SUV.

"Let's go get some ice cream," said Yuri. "That makes everything better, yeah?"

Arm in arm, they walked to the SUV.

Just as Yuri reached for the door handle to let Irina in another black SUV pulled up and two men in dark gray business suits and black sunglasses stepped out. One of them shouted, "Yuri, there's been a development. We need you to test it out."

"Now?" said Yuri, looking to his kids, who were now staring at him with sad expectant faces through the window.

"Now."

Yuri turned to his wife.

"Go," she said, "we'll get the ice cream. Your country needs you."

Yuri couldn't figure out how to interpret that last part as he watched her get in and drive off with the kids, leaving him there alone at the curb.

He turned to the two suits, and said angrily as he walked towards them, "This better be very very important."

"It is Yuri. This might just be the big Journey engine drive breakthrough that we've been hoping for."

Yuri climbed in the rear seat of the SUV and said, "Let me guess, you can't tell me here what it is?"

"That is correct."

"This wouldn't have anything to do with something Carlson may have suggested during his sightseeing tour?"

The two suits exchanged glances, but didn't say a word as they put the SUV into drive.

"That's what I thought. Good ol' Carlson," said Yuri with a knowing laugh. "Let's go see what all the excitement is about."

Part 3 - The Journey Home

Chapter 14 - Location: Silicon Valley, United States

The ride in the black car from the San Jose airport went smoothly. Mike Johnson and Brent Carlson took it mostly in silence.

On the flight back from Moscow, Brent had filled the time by re-reading the Unified Mars Path Papers that he, Shayla, and 11 of his colleagues had worked on 3 years earlier. One passage in particular had stood out for him:

"Want to know what it will take to send humans on their first manned mission to Mars? There has to be a coordinated, multi-nation, multi-commercial organization, multi-NGO, and multi-nonprofit effort to get us there. No single nation or agency can make it happen. We need to be moving forward and looking ahead, while leveraging the existing technology to its utmost capacity. We need to practice excellent planning and execute flawless engineering at the same time. We need to be stoking the fires of public awareness and support for the trip. Only then can we make a human mission to Mars happen. There's only one thing for certain: It won't be easy. But that's never been a good enough reason before to stop us from tackling our toughest challenges." – Brent Carlson, United States Astronaut.

Brent had a smile on his face as he felt the excitement from his adventure around the globe, and let himself hope, just maybe they could pull this off.

Nearing the end of the trip, Brent cleared his throat and said, "I really appreciate you taking me on this trip, Johnson. After going around the world like that, and seeing how excited everyone is, I'm feeling reenergized. Especially after seeing the Journey spacecraft in Hangar 99, things are starting to look up. Ha, no pun intended there."

"Well, you know me, Brent," Johnson replied, "I'm just glad you got to see the fruits of your labors."

"So, I'm assuming we still have one recruit left? The American astronaut." Brent said with an air of expectancy.

"Yes, we do. But I think it's best if we do that one without you."

"Do it without me?" said Brent. "But I thought—"

"You thought what?" Johnson interrupted. "That we were going to ask you to fill the final slot?"

Brent sat back with a sigh.

"You have a top of the charts genius-level IQ," said Johnson. "You can solve some of the most complex multi-variant problems in your head, and yet still, after all these years, I am utterly amazed at how you continually seem to miss the small stuff."

"Wow." Said Brent as he crossed his arms and looked out the window into the distance. "You don't have to be a jerk about it."

"Look, Brent," Johnson said slowly. "Just between you and me, as friends, I can think of no one I would rather have command this mission. No one is better suited or more qualified. But now, as a director of an organization whose top priority is mission assurance, I have to frankly say that there is no way in hell we would ever let you command a mission. You wouldn't be able to pass a psych eval with your alcoholism, your delusions of global conspiracy."

Brent raised an eyebrow at that last bit.

"And you burned far too many bridges with Astronaut Corps and within Congress and further reaches in government. And while nothing you said wasn't technically true, and while there are still those who would follow you to the ends of the Earth and beyond, you simply created far too many enemies to make it even possible at this time."

Brent just looked at Johnson, not saying a word.

"Should I go on?" Johnson asked.

"No, I get it," Brent admitted. "But then, why all this? Why bring me along on the recruiting trip? Besides us being 'friends?' And why not tell me that Ken Solum paid for my trip—and didn't even spring for business class, that billionaire bastard." He punctuated the last statement by mock shaking his fist.

Johnson laughed, and said, "I figured you'd come to that conclusion sooner or later. Look, Brent, you still have a lot of fans out there. You're practically a global icon. You're just too busy trapping yourself in your house and in your bottle to even notice."

"But I haven't had a drop the whole trip," Brent pointed out.

"Yes, but I know you've wanted to the whole trip," Johnson replied. "Even now. I know the look. I've been there, Brent. But here's the rub. You're simply never going back up again as an American astronaut."

Brent let that sink in. He never thought he was going on the trip and he let his hopes rise up. He was right back where he started before the trip. "Can you even be certain we're going to make the launch windows for the Journey?" Brent asked.

"I'm not too certain of any of it," Johnson admitted. "The moon landing took ten years of careful planning, and nothing was really ready until the last two years of it. With the timelines we are working with, the technology exists, but there are so many variables with different countries and different standards for interconnectivity, governmental instability, the list goes on and on."

"Basic project management principles show again and again that the shorter the time to the deadline, the faster the work will get done," said Brent. "Conversely, the longer the time to the deadline, the more perceived effort to achieve the end results. It is just a bit of human nature built in."

"Exactly!" Johnson exclaimed. "Except I don't know if it's time that is the issue."

"And if it's not time, and not technology, then what is it?" Brent asked.

"People," said Johnson. "Is the will of the people strong enough? Mars Journey Program public opinion polls are in the thirty percent range globally. Individual countries rank higher, but without the will of the people..."

"The money runs out, and the technology isn't shared," Brent finished.

"And we're left with billions in expensive technology just floating around in space and sitting on launch pads."

"Level with me here," Brent said. "What do you think our chances are of actually getting this off the ground and making the trip?"

"Officially, we have fifty-fifty odds," Johnson said. "My gut tells me we've got less than a one percent chance of pulling this off without something derailing it. But my optimistic side says there will never be a doubt. Besides, I'm way past retirement age, and I need one final gold star on my record."

"Right, 'cause you do this just for the gold stars," Brent laughed.

"More like the white stars," said Johnson. "The ones on our flag, and the ones out there, too. Well, looks like this is finally our stop."

"Johnson, I really want to thank you," Brent said. "This trip gave me some clarity on what the world looks like. I'm truly going to miss being a part of the mission. It will be hard to not be a part of this anymore. So, thanks."

"You're welcome," Johnson said, looking concerned. "You and Shayla really helped to get this going. It's the least I could do. You sure you're all right?"

"Yeah," said Brent. "Just jet lag setting in, I guess. Either that, or just getting worn down by your company. Just kidding, of course!"

"I know," Johnson said.

As Brent got out of the car, he turned back and added, as an afterthought.

"Hey, Johnson, you never did tell me who they picked as American Commander."

"You sure you want to know?" asked Johnson.

"I'll find out sooner or later, anyways."

Johnson turned to another page in the binder, and flipped it around so Brent could see it.

Brent's eyes went wide. *Williams!* "No. No way. You can't be possibly picking... him!"

"*Yes* way, Brent," Johnson replied. "He's known, after all, for always getting the mission done."

"At any cost," Brent objected. "He's going to be anathema to any esprit de corps that you are going to need on those cramped quarters for your fourteen-month mission."

"He really wasn't selected for his sparkling personality, but for his perseverance. We got this one, Brent. You take care of yourself now. I mean it. My suggestion: clean yourself up. Grab that hidden or not-so-hidden fifth of whatever it is from your bottom desk drawer, or wherever you keep it, and throw it away. You may not be going up as an official astronaut, but I'm sure you have other ways to be a productive member of society... Not sure what they are."

Shaking his head, Brent said, "You got it. Take care, Johnson."

As the black car drove off, Brent turned to face his house. The trip was over. One last hurrah around the planet, so to speak.

Brent went to the mailbox and gathered the usual deliveries. A second month-late notice. Foreclosure eminent notice. Bills and bills... and a large, blue envelope with a gold label. The label read, *Mars Now Needs You.*

Brent shook his head and laughed as he walked into his house.

No, he thought, *you don't need me. After tonight, no one will.*

Chapter 15

That night, Brent got out the bottle of whiskey, sat down at the kitchen counter, poured a tall glass, and put the bottle down next to his wife's photo in frame, resting on top of the pile of mail and bills.

"Right back where we started," Brent said to himself. "I don't think Johnson is coming to interrupt this time around," he finished with a sigh.

Brent took the photo out of the frame, and started talking to Shayla as if she were there. "I keep feeling like I'm just away on one of my missions, and I'll be coming back to see you soon, thought Brent. That's how I'm wired. And I can't seem to unwire it. In my heart, I keep expecting to see you again… but I never will. Well. Not on this plane of existence. Guess we're about to find out if we will on the next."

He placed the photo down, reached into the table drawer, and wrapped his hand around the grip of his M9 Beretta pistol. It was a matching version of the one he'd worn as a sidearm as a member of the Stealth Scorpion Taskforce in the Army. It didn't have the greatest stopping power or the highest accuracy, but it was efficient, effective, and once you found a weapon you liked, you tended to stick with it.

He looked forlornly into the drawer, sighed aloud, and then looked behind him at the plastic tarp he had spread to cover the counter and the floor behind him. It wasn't his best work, but it should do the trick. He picked up the photo.

"Goodbye, my love," he said. "I will see you soon."

He kissed the image of Shayla, and put the photo face down on the table. He raised the drink to his mouth with his free left hand. Rested the glass on his lips. Hating that smell. Hating himself. But needing the liquid courage to go through with his escape plan.

He looked up at the mirror, inhaling before imbibing.

What he saw in the mirror made his blood run cold and the hair stand up on the back of his neck.

The mirror reflected the window above the kitchen sink.

There was a pair of eyes peering in at him through the dark!

Chapter 16

Brent slowly lowered the drink to the table and squinted at the mirror. Quick as a flash, he drew the M9 and turned, pointing the weapon at the window. Nothing. His military training returning to him in an instant, he darted to the back door, flung it open, and jumped out sidelong, two hands on the gun as he shouted, "Stop! Identify yourself!"

Nothing. Silence. Crickets and birds on a quarter-moon night.

Glancing left and right across the yard, the only thing he saw was his tool shed that housed the ride-on mower and power tools for the household projects he never completed.

His adrenaline spike was beginning to taper. The feeling of jitters started to form in his legs, and he lowered the gun.

"Anyone out here?" he called out.

HOO! HOO! Answered an owl.

Brent laughed out loud and turned towards the woods and said, "Why thank you, Mr. Owl. Your mock is well received. Jesus, Carlson. The things you invent to keep yourself from killing yourself."

Grinning still, his eyes settled on the soft, almost imperceptible orange line emanating from under his shed doors. He froze. Had he turned that light on? How long had it been since he'd been in there?

Should I call the cops? he thought. What would I say? There is a light in my shed, and I'm scared?

The light flicked off.

That's not good. Either I'm imagining things, or someone is about to get a bullet in them.

Grin gone, Brent proceeded towards the shed.

He reached out with one hand for the latch, his other hand holding the gun. He flung the doors open.

"Identify yourself, or I will shoot!"

Nothing.

The low light of the quarter moon barely helped Brent Carlson make out the shapes in the garage. Ride-on mower. Power tools. Two-by-fours. His eyes darting left and right. Suddenly, he became painfully aware that he didn't have a flashlight. His hand shot into the shed and flicked on the light switch. Light filled the ten-by-ten space, but there was nothing. He ducked down, but saw no one under the bench.

"Jesus, Carlson," he said aloud, again. He lowered the gun. "What is wrong with you?"

He turned to leave, his hand reaching out to turn off the light, but he froze in mid-motion when the little voice inside his head said: Look up.

Shifting his gaze upward, to the ceiling of the A-frame shed, he found himself staring at a man dressed all in black with a black mask on, crouched in the rafters, only his eyes showing, looking down at Brent.

Not wasting words, Brent raised the gun to shoot. The other man came diving down feet first, catching Brent on the hand. A shot firing off into the night with a *crack*, and the gun hurtled to the floor.

The man in black punched straight and hard towards Brent's face, causing Brent's guard to come up instinctually. This left his mid-section open, a space which the assailant filled with a driving side kick, knocking the air out of Brent's lungs and sending him flying back. His spine made contact with the cornered edge of the mower's grill. Shocked and out of breath, he barely had time to bring his arms together to block a hard punch aimed at his solar plexus, leaving his neck exposed, and the man in black sunk in a guillotine grip.

Amazing, how time slows down, Brent thought as the life was being squeezed out of him, and the thoughts you have when the blood and oxygen to your brain are cut off... He set me up for the choke with a mid-section strike. This guy is good. Real good. And I'm apparently really out of shape. And apparently, I am going out.

He started to drift from consciousness when he had a piercing thought.

This guy knows who killed Shayla. This guy might be the one who killed Shayla!

Willpower trumped biological physiology, and suddenly, there was life again. And rage. Brent had been an all-American wrestler, a BJJ brown belt, and a skilled kickboxing practitioner. None of the mental know -how mattered now, as rage unconsciously selected the tools to be used.

A driving knee to the groin. No loosening of the neck grip, but it created a little space between Brent and his assailant. Another driving knee aimed at the man's solar plexus. This one lifted him in the air a bit and definitely loosened his grip. Now, Brent dropped down, pulling the man in black off balance. His center of gravity shifted over Brent, and Brent shot all his power straight up in the air. At full extension, Brent brought the man in black crashing backwards, face first into the engine cover of the mower, and the grip was broken.

Face broken, too, hopefully, thought Brent as he rolled to his right, onto his knees, then back to his feet in time to see the man dart from the shed, holding his face.

Not fast enough. You're mine!

Brent pursued like a cheetah in lithe, powerful sprint, leaping into the air, hands finding purchase in the clothing to both sides of the neck of his prey. Still in the air, Brent brought the insteps of his feet to the back of the man in black's knees, driving his two hundred pounds of mass into them, forcing them to the ground. Brent heard the loud pop of ligaments tearing, and a scream let out from the man in black's mouth.

"Oh no, you don't," Brent said, as he swung his arm under the assailant's neck, putting him in a choke position from behind with full leverage. "First, I'm going to choke you out, and then, I'm going to wake you up with some very pointed questions..."

A noise from the shed reversed Brent's focus. He turned his head just in time to see another man, dressed all in black, swinging a two-by-four at his head.

Two of them. Great!

It was all he had a chance to think before his lights went out.

Chapter 17

Brent stood outside his shed, holding an ice pack to his head. Brent had been giving his account to the cops for some time now.

They didn't believe him.

"You have a history of making crazy claims," an officer said.

"But the assault?" responded Brent. "The two-by-four?"

"We found only *your* fingerprints on the two-by-four," said the cop.

"And the bruises?"

"Sorry to say, but they are easily faked," the cop maintained.

"And the surveillance cameras?" Brent asked.

"Turned off," the cop stated. "Remotely. And only you have the password, correct?"

"That could be easily hacked," Brent replied.

"Look, you shot a gun off randomly into the air," the cop said angrily. "Thank God no one got hurt. You have what looks to be a suicide in progress in the kitchen, and we found this crazy, serial killer-like shrine to some guy named Herr Graden in your basement. The only reason we are not arresting you right now is because some people high up made some phone calls to my boss' boss' boss. Your neighbors are scared to death of you. We are confiscating your weapon. You are out of chances. If we have one more report of ninjas or boogey men or anything, I don't care who you are, or who calls who, I will put you in the cell myself."

Brent was speechless and just stared in stunned disbelief.

"Do you understand?" the cop demanded.

"I do," Brent answered. "Are we done here?"

"We are."

"Good. Now get off my property!"

Chapter 18

Brent sat down at the table. His gun was gone, now. The glass of whiskey was still sitting there. Brent just stared at it, shaking his head.

"*RAHHHHH*" he shouted at the ceiling, at the stars, at the gods.

He slammed his fist down on the table. The glass of whiskey spilled over and ran towards his stack of mail.

"No, no, no, no," he said as he automatically went to grab a towel to blot the alcohol.

He moved the stack of bills and letters over to the counter. When he plopped them down, one fell out onto the floor, the blue letter with *Mars Now Needs You* emblazoned in gold. The words seemed to stare up at him from the floor.

"What is this nonsense?" Brent picked up the envelope, tore it open, and pulled out a one-way ticket to Australia. Also in the envelope was a handwritten note.

Dear Brent Carlson, read the letter. This is the 10th letter we have written you. Since you submitted your application a year ago, you have been routinely advanced to the next levels of competition. You are currently ranked #1 in the world, and therefore are the first choice for the Journey Program Partnership. We require you to respond to this letter and meet with us within one week of its postmark or your posting will be forfeit.

Brent checked the postmark. "Hmm. That's in two days…"

The letter went on: We are aware of your stature as a former American astronaut and co-architect of the United Path to Mars Plan, and therefore, we would like to offer you special consideration.

Kindly, Dr. Stuffert and Mr. Jensen

"That actually sounds promising," said Brent.

He went to throw the envelope and its contents off to the side when the soothing voice of Shayla in his head spoke to him and said *Connect the pieces.*

He froze. His eyes locked on some distant unseen point. *It was happening again. Better just strap in for the ride.*

His mind revved up to higher and higher cycles. Brent felt like he was no longer in that room. He was in his mind, his beautiful, unique, powerful, problem-solving mind. Images of Shayla, Johnson, Andrea, Yuri, Li, Ken Solum, Herr Graden, and the Journey swirled, and expanded. He saw Earth, and off over the horizon, a red blur, and he was hurtling towards it. The blur gained focus and clarity and it was Mars, and they were flying by it, and he was on the ship, and they were all dead.

And suddenly, it all went in reverse and increased to triple speed, then ten times speed, all the way back to Earth, all the way to the present.

What went wrong?

Backwards, Brent went through pain, struggle, riots, celebrations, as if billions of voices spoke out all at once, backwards, and then forwards again to Mars, and back to where he was, in this room.

Fix it!

Again and again, faster and faster.

Modify that!

The technology flashed in and out of focus, and Brent caught glimpses, remembering all he could, small changes and big changes. He hovered in the space between worlds, godlike, seeing the connections, the powers, the streams of energy, and the visible pull of gravity. Finally, at impossible speeds, Brent flew forward, until Mars filled his vision, and he was hurtling towards the surface. Before impact, he realized he was standing on Mars with Earth looming impossibly large on the horizon. He looked down at his feet, standing on red soil, and up at the blue dot against the backdrop of black.

This is the way.

And then, all went black, and Brent dropped to his knees, exhausted.

After a few minutes, Brent regained his feet. He wasn't sure how long he had been like that, but the clock on the wall told him that it had been at least an hour. It was getting late.

Brent had gone into powerful mental trances like this ever since he was a kid. Usually under stress and pressure his higher cognitive functions kicked into overdrive. His parents used to worry about him, but Brent learned to use it like a tool. He hadn't gone into a mental trance like that for some time. Last time he had, was when he concluded that Herr Graden was behind the conspiracy to murder his wife. He could only surmise that maybe the alcohol was keeping his brain suppressed, and this last week of clarity allowed him to tap into that state again.

He put the ticket and envelope down on the table next to the photo of Shayla. He picked up the bottle of whiskey and walked to the sink, emptying its contents down the drain. He picked up his cell phone as he stumbled to his bedroom and hit the speed dial for Lawrence.

"Jesus, Brent," Lawrence answered on the other end. "It's one in the morning! I heard about the cops. Do you need me to come over?"

"Just come in the morning," Brent replied.

"You drunk?" asked Lawrence, sounding worried. "You okay?"

"See you at nine. Crashing."

Brent hit the button to hang up, faced the bed, and crash-landed onto it. He was out before he even settled in.

Chapter 19

Lawrence arrived at Brent's house at nine the next morning. He had a key but didn't need to use it. The front door was wide open.

Lawrence entered through the front door. He and Brent had been friends together since they were kids, and he had gotten used to Brent's crazy ideas. But the state of this house had him worried. It looked like a bomb had gone off.

Brent appeared in front of him with a stack of papers in his hands, having come up out of the basement.

"I need you to sell the house," Brent told him. "Use any profit to cover your fees. Get this place cleaned out. Anything in the basement and on the memory shelf in the living room, have sent to storage. Please oversee that personally, and if there is anything left over, get me a camper or something, will ya?"

Lawrence stared with his mouth agape and could only let out, "Uh, sure thing, Brent. You okay, buddy?"

"Better than I've been in a long time."

"Care to elaborate?" Lawrence asked.

Brent's face grew sad. "I'm tired of running. I'm tired of hiding. And I'm tired of drinking myself to death. I'm tired of not being the person I was meant to be. I was going to kill myself last night, Lawrence. Like, really do it."

"Brent! I... I had no idea."

"I'm not telling you for pity or as a cry for help," Brent said slowly. "I was going to do it. Then, when I was attacked by the man in black, I found myself fighting for my life. And that just didn't compute. Why would I fight for my life when I was about to end it? That's like a glitch in the Matrix, and for me, it was like a reboot of the system."

"A fresh start?" Lawrence suggested.

"Something like that, yeah," Brent said. "I realized that it's time for me to make my move before I lose all my resources and credibility."

"I know what you want," said Lawrence. "I've known that for years. But sometimes, the world isn't ready. Sometimes, it's not enough to want to be a better person. Or to be a better species."

"It's way beyond that, Lawrence," said Brent, raising his voice. "It's not just about feel-good achievement. It's about the very survival of our species on our planet."

Lawrence was a bit shocked at Brent's ferocity. Brent picked up a small, globe-shaped paperweight from the table and tossed it back and forth from one hand to the other. He took a deep, calming breath before continuing.

"There's a law of progress that affects our lives. If you're not active, you atrophy. If you're not learning, you're getting dumber. If you're not progressing, you're dying. It's a forward-moving drive that can be found in all life forms, not just ours, and it can be found at higher and higher levels of systems, such as our global human presence."

"That's a liberal mix of motivation and ecosystem theory there, but I'm following," said Lawrence.

"We're on an undeniable collision course unless something drastic happens. All the signs of it abound, if you just know how to look for it, much like you can find black holes by observing the space, time, and gravity that warps around them. Well, we have much that is warping around us, all the death and decay and disease and destruction all around us. Millions of species are dying off. We're killing ourselves and the only home we have. And that's because we stopped progressing as a species in one critical area."

"But we have access to better education, and homes, and cars, and luxury items," said Lawrence. "Surely you have to recognize that."

"Those are economic indicators, and they tell only a fraction of the story. It is in our very human nature—in our DNA—to explore, and we've run out of places to explore on this planet. What happens when you put wild chimpanzees in a zoo?"

"They get depressed and bored."

"That's us. We are caged chimpanzees. Caged lions. And we hate our captors, and we hate ourselves for letting us be captured. And I don't know precisely why or how I know, but I know with every fabric of my being that human exploration and habitation of Mars is the path to the next level of evolution for our species. It is the catalyst for raising the collective consciousness of our planet, and it is the vital element leading to the survival of our species, setting us free from our current doomsday course."

At that, Brent set down the globe, grabbed a hybrid map and spreadsheet from the table, and held it up for Lawrence to see. Patterns crisscrossed the continents. The word Focusing Lens was drawn across the top in black marker. Along the side, there were names and titles that Lawrence was just able to make out before Brent lowered it: *The leader, the celebrity, the martyr.*

"That looks like a pretty complicated map," Lawrence said.

"It's actually a key," Brent said. "The key to everything." He folded it and put it in his back pocket.

"Everything, huh?" Lawrence said, unsure of whether his friend had finally snapped or if he was actually starting to understand, for the first time, what Brent had been after all along. "And what is all of this?" he said, pointing to the luggage stacked up at the door, hoping to change the subject. "It looks like you're set to head out on quite the journey."

"The longest Journey, I would say," Brent commented, picking up his wife's photo from the table, folding it, and putting it in his back pocket. "I'm headed to the airport, Lawrence. And from there, Australia, and from there... I'm not quite sure. But I do know what I need to do now. Correction. I know what I am *going* to do."

"And what's that, Brent?"

"I am going to get us to Mars, and I won't stop unless it kills me. And even then..." Brent's voice trailed off.

"And just how are *you* going to do that?"

"Sometimes, it's not about *how* you get something done. It's about *how bad* do you want it."

With a slight grin on Brent's face, the one that meant he was about to get into some mischief or trouble or both, he turned and walked out the door. Lawrence watched him leave, too shocked to say anything else and knowing too well that nothing he could say would stop Brent. Of all his friends, of all his legal clients, heck, of all the people he knew, that man just might have been the craziest. He was also the only one Lawrence knew of who could actually make good on a promise like that.

Chapter 20 - Location: Northern California Mountain Wilderness, United States

The pickup truck careened down the dirt road, brushing up against tree branches that whipped the antenna back and forth smacking off the windshield. Two men, one tall and the other short, dressed in black combat gear from head to toe were tossed back and forth in the cab as the vehicle took the curves hard. The truck took the crest at high velocity, and all four wheels left the ground. The man in the passenger seat shouted as his head hit the roof of the cab.

"Jesus, slow down!" Shouted Kato, the shorter of the two. "This is killing my leg."

"Sorry," said Walker, "but maybe you should be wearing your seatbelt or something."

"You're going to kill us!"

"You almost got us killed last night! The boss said we were just supposed to keep an eye on him. Only approach if someone were trying to do him harm."

"Well, you didn't see what I saw, and now I've got to get surgery and rehab on this leg to thank for my efforts. Look out!"

Walker slammed the breaks hard as a deer ran out in front of them. The truck came to sliding halt, kicking dust and rocks up in the air.

"Come on, Walker! I told you to slow down!"

"Relax, we're here."

The truck stopped in front of an eight-foot-high barbed wire fence enclosure surrounding an eighty-foot cell phone tower. Walker cut the engine, trotted around to Kato's side of the truck, and helped him out. They hobbled together to the gate, thumbed the combination lock open, and locked it behind them before making their way to an access hatch in the side of the tower. The doorway was barely large enough for Walker to squeeze through. Kato, the smaller of the two descended quickly despite his injury.

Walker punched in the key code, and they both entered the underground communications bunker. Servers whirred and hummed, and flashing lights signaled the transference of terabytes of data.

"This place shouldn't exist," said Kato.

"Well, it does. Let's get this call with the boss over with and get the heck out before someone else notices we're here."

Kato hopped on one leg over to the phone console and slumped in the chair next to it. "How do you think he'll know to call us—?"

The phone rang.

"There's all kinds of sensor in here and outside," Walker said as he leaned in and picked up the phone. "Delta, Hotel, Alpha, Kilo, five, eight, Foxtrot, Zulu, seven," he spoke into the phone and waited for voice confirmation. "Yes, sir, we are secure. I'll put you on speaker."

Walker reached out and flicked the speakerphone switch.

"What in the nine hells happened out there?" came a deep voice, distorted and processed through a voice modulator.

Walker and Kato just looked at each other.

"Well?" the voice demanded.

Walker pointed to Kato and mouthed the words, "Speak up."

"Things got crazy, sir," said Kato.

"Things weren't supposed to get crazy. You guys are professionals. You're Atlas Force for Christ's sake! Your job was to observe and protect, and from what I can tell from the networked police reports, you nearly killed him."

"Walker nearly killed him," said Kato.

"Yeah, because you were getting your butt handed to you," Walker cut in.

"Enough. It's like talking to a bunch of children out there. How did Carlson spot you?"

"You're not going to like this, sir," said Kato, "but Carlson was about to do himself in."

"You mean... kill himself?"

"Yes sir. I had to stop him somehow. I blew my cover, and the rest was just the fallout."

"Damn. I guess I should have seen that coming."

"That guy is like a one-man wrecking crew," said Kato.

"I know he is," said the modulated voice. "You're lucky to be alive. Where is he now?"

"Gone," said Walker. "We swung back this morning after we laid low the rest of the night, and his place is cleared out."

"Wait, what? Someone came and got him?"

"No, sir. From what we can tell, he left on his own."

"And you have no idea where he is?"

"None, sir," said Kato. "I'm sure you can track him if you have access to your old deep search systems."

"I don't, unfortunately. Until he pops back up, you guys go back to your normal routines."

"I don't get it, though," said Walker. "I know he's an astronaut, and we've been watching over him for a long time, but why is this guy so important?"

"Can't say over this line. I appreciate you working this one. I owe you."

The line when silent, and Kato flipped the speaker switch off. "Can't say over this secure line? This might be the last time I agree to help you out with a favor from an old buddy."

"Yeah, like you have a choice right? But I agree, this one is a little too much over my pay grade. Let's get you to a medic."

Chapter 21

The man at the other end of the line sat staring at the phone, slowly shaking his head and rubbing his chin in contemplation.

What have I gotten myself into?

He slid the voice modulator into the desk drawer and stood up. He punched in a code on the keypad on the desk, disengaging the security protocols. Blackout panels retreated from in front of the windows. The red light over the door blinked out and turned green.

With a heavy sigh, he walked to the window, opened the blinds, and looked out over the streets of Washington DC. The lunch trucks had pulled up on the streets, and his employees were gathering below.

So oblivious, he thought. *I guess that's a good thing. They have no idea what's coming. That's why I do what I do.*

"Yeah, keep telling yourself that," he said aloud.

He walked to the mirror and straightened his already straight tie with the absentminded practice of someone who had been performing that motion for a very long time.

"Think I'll get out today and grab me something from the lunch truck," he said into the mirror, and let himself smile a little. "Will be good to get out among my people."

Ignorant bliss. Momentary reprieve, at least.

He walked to the door, released the deadbolt, and stepped outside into the hustle and bustle of a busy office. He was immediately approached by his secretary.

"You have three messages, sir, and the ESA Administration office has been holding on line two for 30 minutes."

"Thanks, Rebecca. I'm going to have to take those when I get back."

"But the ESA will be closed by the time you get back…"

"I said hold my calls!" he snapped.

Rebecca sank back, trying to hide her shock.

"Sorry about that, Rebecca. I need to take a walk, grab some lunch, and clear my head. I've got a lot on my mind."

"No worries, sir. I understand. There is a lot of pressure on you."

He forced a smile and walked off.

You have no idea what pressure I am under, young lady. I'm just glad you don't know what is coming, and how little there is we can do about it. Going to forget about this for a minute. Grab a street taco from the lunch truck.

He made it halfway down the hall when he heard Rebecca call after him, "Administrator Johnson! Sir, I know you said to hold your calls... but it's Ken Solum. He says it's urgent. I can take a message if you like."

"No, that's fine, Rebecca," he said as he turned back towards her. "I'll take the call at my desk."

"Yes, sir."

Johnson re-entered his office, closed the door behind him, reached for the secure panel switches, and thought, *guess I don't get a momentary reprieve when the very fate of the world is resting on my decisions, and getting to Mars is one of the best shots we have for the survival of the species. How in the hell did it come to this?*

Chapter 22

The End Of Book 1... The Epic Journey Continues in Book 2

Thank you for reading Mars Journey: Call to Action – Book 1. I hope you enjoyed it as much as I enjoyed writing it.

The Mars Journey series will take us from the beginning with the space station disaster that you just read, the effort to get the crew to the launch, the journey through space, and hopefully make it to Mars (it is a long and dangerous mission after all). I look forward to continuing the journey with you.

Ad Mars et Ultra (To Mars and Beyond),

William Strong

About the Author

William Strong is the USA Today bestselling author of the near-future science fiction thriller series - Mars Journey: Call to Action. When William was 8 years old, he was wrongfully committed to a mental institution for 3 years for a crime he didn't commit.

William turned to reading Stephen King and the Hardy Boys series as an escape, and when he was 13 he began writing his own stories of heroes fighting villains and overcoming incredible odds. Now William is a US Army Veteran, a former Fortune 500 Chief Technologist, and a successful entrepreneur. He draws upon his technical expertise and experiential living to bring life to his characters and stories.

William has been featured in CIO, the Huffington Post, and the Washington Post. He writes side by side with his wife, author Daniele Love, and their two cats: Frankie and Kitty. Get timely updates on William's books and other projects at
http://williamstrong.com